these top **tips** turn you into a super soccer player! **Memorize** them, **believe** in them, and **practice** them. That's still the best tip of all: to be **good** at anything, you must practice, practice, practice!

Meet the ball.

Never stand and wait
for the ball to come to you.
Always run to meet it.

The ball is your friend.

Take the ball with you everywhere you can. Play with it all the time— while you wait for the bus, while you walk with a friend. **The better you get to know the ball, the better you will play.**

Introduce the ball ● to your feet.

Your **instep** will kick the ball with surprising power.

The **sole** of your foot will stop the ball on a dime.

● They can play tricks together.

Your **heel** will go into reverse and pass behind you.

The **sides** of your feet will make passes.

Learn to juggle. ●

Juggling is fun, and it will build you

● Bounce the ball using your feet, legs, chest, and head. Try not to let it hit the ground.

coordination, balance, and control.

Look like a klutz. ●

If you are right-handed, practice everything with your left foot first. If you are left-handed, use your right foot.

● It will **improve your coordination.**

You'll be surprised how
easy things seem when you
finally switch feet.

Look even more like a klutz. ●

Try to play with your hands in your pockets. You will **learn the importance of good balance**.

Learn to use your head.*

Practice by gently bouncing a Nerf ball off your forehead. It will help you **locate the right spot** for heading the ball.

*Be smart. Never try to head a ball without talking to your coach first and learning the proper technique.

Have faith in your ability.

It's natural to be nervous about trying
a new skill. But you can do it!
It just takes practice. **Talk to your
coach** about your concerns.
He or she will help you decide
when you're ready to go for it.

Make mistakes. ●

Only one of three pass

will go where you want it to.

Pass anyway.
You should
**always pass if
you can.**

Be sneaky.

Don't look at the player
you're passing to.
Surprise your opponent.

It's impossible. But you should always **keep your head up** and watch the field. And **watch the ball** at your feet too.

t once. (Or try.)

Practice! Try to balance a book on your head while you kick the ball. You'll see just how much your head moves!

Try to play . . .
with a tennis ball.

If you can dribble well with a tennis ball

a soccer ball should seem easy!

Turn your body into a pillow.

To trap the ball, you need to **cushion it.** If you can act like a pillow, you'll do very well.

Listen for the whistle.

Play to the whistle,

not to what you see happen.

The referee can miss a play,

but the game will continue

until the whistle blows.

Be confident.

Never hesitate. **Take your best shot.**
It won't work all the time, but that's
what the team is for—to help out.

And don't forget to:

Warm up.

Wear shin guards.

Practice the basics.

Keep moving at all times.

Take chances.

Love the game.